Three Little Kittens

For Jamie, Jacob, Nathaniel, and Mariska

Clarion Books
a Houghton Mifflin Company imprint
215 Park Avenue South, New York, NY 10003
Copyright © 1986 by Paul Galdone
For information about permission to reproduce
selections from this book, write to Permissions,
Houghton Mifflin Company, 215 Park Avenue South, New York, NY 10003.
Manufactured in China
Library of Congress Cataloging-in-Publication Data. Galdone, Paul. Three little kittens.
Summary: Three little kittens lose, find, soil, and wash their mittens. 1. Nursery rhymes.
2. Children's poetry.
[1. Cats—Poetry. 2. Nursery rhymes] I. Title. PZ8.3.G1218Th 1986
398′.8 86-2655
LEO 40 39
4500221239
CL ISBN-13: 978-0-89919-426-4 CL ISBN-10: 0-89919-426-5
PA ISBN-13: 978-0-89919-796-8 PA ISBN-10: 0-89919-796-5

Three Little Kittens

Illustrated by
PAUL GALDONE

CLARION BOOKS
NEW YORK

Three

Little Kittens

they lost their
mittens,
and they began
to cry,

"Oh, Mother Dear, we sadly fear
Our mittens we have lost!"

7

"What! lost your mittens,
you naughty kittens!

9

Then you shall have no pie."

10

The
three little kittens

12

found their mittens
and they began to cry,

13

"Oh! Mother Dear, see here, see here.
Our mittens we have found."

"What!
found your mittens,
you good little kittens,

15

Then you shall have some pie." "Purr, purr, purr."

17

The three little kittens

put on their mittens
and soon ate up the pie.

"Oh! Mother Dear, we greatly fear
Our mittens we have soiled."

Then they
began to sigh,
"Meow,
meow,
meow!"

23

The three little kittens

washed their mittens,

and hung them up to dry.

"Oh! Mother Dear,
look here, look here

Our mittens
we have
washed."

"What! washed your mittens,
you darling kittens!

But
hush!
I smell
a rat
close
by."

"Yes, we smell a rat close by.
Meow, meow, *meow!*"